Library of Congress Cataloging-in-Publication Data is available.

iSBN 978-0-06-207750-9 (trade bdg.)

16   SCP   10 9 8 7 6 5 4 3

First American Edition

Originally published in Great Britain by HarperCollins Children's Books in 2010.

FOR Sue and Judith . SB ★

★ special thanks to Wayne .

TOOT and POP!

Sebastien Braun

HARPER

An Imprint of HarperCollinsPublishers

This is Pop. Hello, Pop!

He is a very strong little tugboat.

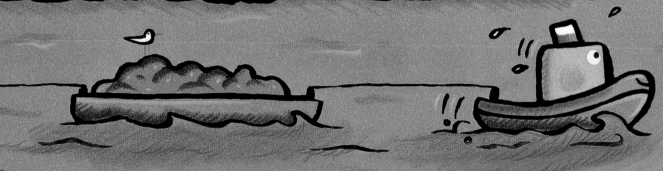

Every day Pop works in the harbor,
pulling all the big, heavy loads.

"Heave-ho!"

Then he guides all the great
big boats safely out to sea.

"Pop!

Pop!

Pop!"

he says.
"Follow me!"

One day, a brand-new boat was being
launched in the harbor.

Pop couldn't wait to see it. He rushed off to the dock . . .

and what a boat it was!

"You are **enormous,**" gasped Pop.
"I know!" said the new boat.
"**I'm Toot.**"
He sounded his horn proudly.

"**TOOT!**"

"*You!*" exclaimed Toot.
"I'm big and strong. I don't need help
from anyone, especially you!"

Huge waves swirled behind him, rocking and
knocking all the boats into one another.
"Watch out!" yelled Lenny the lighthouse.
But it was too late. . . .

"TOOT!"

Toot ran straight into the seawall and came to a stop. His engine was broken.

The harbormaster
hurried over.
"Silly Toot!" he said.
"Look what you've done."

"He wouldn't wait
for Pop," said Lenny.

"Well, now you'll just have
to let Pop take you back to
the dock to be fixed," the
harbormaster told Toot sternly.

No sooner had he spoken than Pop came rushing to the rescue.

Soon Toot was settled in the dock, ready to be fixed.

"I'm sorry, Pop," he said. "I should have let you do your job.

Please will you help me when I'm back in the water?"

"Of course I will," said Pop kindly. . . .

Pop sailed happily back
across the harbor.
"Well done, Pop!" said Lenny.

"It's all in a day's work," said Pop.